For my parents

The Blue Jackal

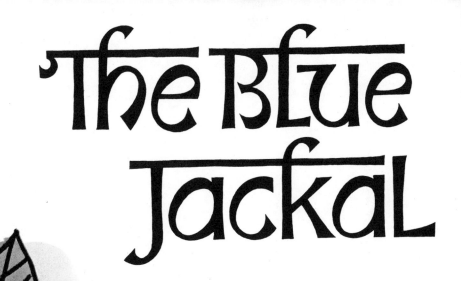

Retold and illustrated by

MEHLLI GOBHAI

Prentice-Hall, Inc., Englewood Cliffs, N.J.

THE BLUE JACKAL   Retold and illustrated by Mehlli Gobhai   © 1968 by Mehlli Gobhai

Library of Congress Catalog Card Number: 68-11099   Printed in the United States of America   J 07769

Prentice-Hall International, Inc., London   Prentice-Hall of Australia, Pty. Ltd., Sydney   Prentice-Hall of Canada, Ltd., Toronto   Prentice-Hall of India Private Ltd., New Delhi   Prentice-Hall of Japan, Inc., Tokyo

At the edge of a deep, green forest near a small village in India, lived a timid jackal named Long Howl. He spent most of his time hiding in a cave because he was afraid of all the other animals.

Sometimes Long Howl dreamed terrible dreams. He imagined he was being stalked by a huge tiger with sharp, cruel claws.

The only time Long Howl was not afraid was when he joined the jackal pack at twilight for their evening song. He felt almost important then, since he could howl louder and longer than any other jackal.

Long Howl often went hungry because he was afraid to hunt for his dinner. One evening, he had been without food all day and his empty belly rumbled.

He crept up quite close to the village market-place and hid in a thicket. From the huts came a wonderful aroma of *kofta* and *khichdi*, stewing in herbs and spices.

Two children were munching sugar cane. Ah, if only he could have a taste!

Just then, a large, fierce dog sprang to his feet with a snarl. He had caught a whiff of the hidden jackal . . .

Suddenly, all the village dogs gave chase.
Long Howl ran for his life.

Now the jackal was only a few feet ahead of the snapping jaws. He dodged into the courtyard of a dyer's home. Freshly dyed *saris* whipped his face as he galloped past them.

Using the last of his strength, Long Howl gathered himself for a leap. With a great splash he landed smack in the middle of a vat of indigo blue dye.

Poor Long Howl almost choked on the dye. It ran into his eyes and out of his ears. But he dared not cough or sneeze with the dogs so close.

He crouched down at the bottom of the vat. His body was covered by the cool, wet blue dye, which was bright as the wings of the kingfisher.

The dogs whined and sniffed all around the vat but they could find no trace of Long Howl. Finally, the dogs felt sure that the jackal had escaped and they trotted off.

When all was still, Long Howl lifted his nose above the rim of the vat. He sniffed all around. The smell of the dogs was far away. Now his eyes were above the rim and there was not a dog in sight.

Long Howl heard voices. They were coming closer. The dyer's family came into the courtyard to take the dry *saris* from the line. Imagine their surprise when they saw a bright blue beast leap from one of the vats.

The whole family began shouting . . .

Long Howl had but one thought—escape. He ran for his forest home as fast as his long legs could carry him.

The other animals were even more surprised than the people when they saw the strange blue animal.

"Perhaps he has poison fangs," thought the tiger. "How hard can he strike and how sharp are his nails?" worried the tender rabbits.

"Could the god Indra himself have sent this fierce blue animal to rule over us?" wondered the clever monkeys.

So, to be on the safe side, all the animals fled from Long Howl's presence.

When all the animals had run away, Long Howl sat under a banyan tree and thought.

He was indeed pleased that some of the largest and strongest and cleverest animals in the forest seemed to be afraid of him.

Long Howl took a deep breath. His chest swelled and he began to feel very fine and fierce.

Since all the animals were afraid of him, Long Howl decided to make himself their king. He soon became proud and bossy.

He made the tiger his prime minister and the peacock his messenger. The monkeys took turns fanning him and all the animals had to kneel before speaking to him.

He commanded his subjects to bring him lots of the most delicious foods—juicy mangoes, stacks of sugar cane, and mounds of fresh mice.

Only the jackals would not bow down to King Long Howl. They did not want a jackal for their king, so they moved to another part of the forest.

One night, King Long Howl was sitting on his favorite knoll. Sometimes he liked to be by himself and away from his humble subjects.

Just then, the quiet night air was pierced by the terrible wail of the jackal pack. They had come back to their favorite hunting grounds.

The screeches and wails of the jackal pack reached the kingly ears of Long Howl. These were sounds he simply could not resist. The urge to answer his brother jackals became very strong.

Long Howl forgot that he was king of the beasts. He pointed his muzzle at the newly-risen moon and howled the loudest, longest howl of his entire life.

When the other animals heard the jackal-howl being howled by their king, they were deeply shocked.

They came running and creeping and flying out of the forest. Suddenly, all of them could clearly see the jackal body under the bright indigo coat. It made them very cross to learn they had been fooled.

Snarling and hissing and screeching, they bore down upon Long Howl and chased him away.

The blue jackal was king no longer.

Once more Long Howl must hunt for his own food. He still wears his indigo coat but it is fading.

Soon he will be his own true color again. Perhaps then the jackal pack will let Long Howl join them for their evening song.

Meanwhile, in India, people tell of a blue jackal who sits alone as night falls and howls—the longest, saddest howl ever heard.

ABOUT THE STORY

The Blue Jackal is an ancient fable. It was written in Sanskrit, the classical Indian language, about two hundred years B.C. Scholars believe that the story of the blue jackal was ancient even then.

The story is part of a collection of eighty-four tales called the *Panchatantra,* or five books. The *Panchatantra* is an anthology of *niti,* or stories dealing with the wise conduct of life.

According to legend, the *Panchatantra* was written by a Brahmin, a holy man named Vishnu-sharman. He composed it in order to help educate the three foolish sons of a wise rajah.

The *Panchatantra* stories have appeared all over the world in many different versions. One of the earliest printed collections was an English adaptation run off by William Caxton. A free German translation of the *Panchatantra* was one of the first books to be printed in medieval Europe.

WHAT THE INDIAN WORDS MEAN

BANYAN: From the Indian word *banya,* meaning "merchant." The English named this fig tree banyan when they first saw merchants set up a marketplace in its shade. These trees have branches that grow sprouts which take root and become new trunks. Very old banyans can shelter as many as a thousand people.

INDRA: The ancient king of the gods, ruler of the lofty sky, whose weapon is a thunderbolt.

KHICHDI: Lentils and rice.

KOFTA: Meatballs made from mutton.

SARI: Usually six yards of cotton or silk draped in various ways. This is the traditional dress of Indian Women.